A LOWCOUNTRY CHRISTMAS MIRACLE

Christmas Miracle Series: VOLUME 3

Sandy Loyd

Miracles have a way of happening at Christmastime. The miracle of family coming together, the miracle of forgiveness, and the most wonderful miracle of all, the miracle of finding true love.

Chapter 1

The dogs ran alongside the three-wheeler as Madelyn Duval steered around a deep hole in the ground. Suddenly, Rock and Roll began barking wildly and spinning around in circles. Madelyn came to a complete stop.

"Good boys," she said, hopping out. As trained, they'd locked onto the boar's scent and were waiting for her command. "Go get 'im," she yelled.

Rock took off for the bushes. Roll was fast on his tail. Madelyn grabbed her rifle out of the vehicle and followed, struggling to keep up through the South Carolina shrubs and palmetto trees.

Snarling and barking filled the air, along with loud squealing.

Madelyn cocked her rifle and ran the rest of the way. Her dogs were well-trained for hunting, but a boar could do damage and her dogs were too stupid to realize it. When close enough to take a shot, she whistled.

"Heel, boys."

They immediately obeyed. Once they were out of the line of fire, she aimed at the charging boar, hitting him right between the eyes.

"Jesus, Mother. Why do you take chances like that?"

She lowered the rifle and spun around to face her oldest son, who'd obviously followed her. "If I waited for one of you all to take care of him, I wouldn't have a garden left, now would I?" Her nod indicated the boar's carcass. "Take care of him for me. Will you?"

Martin grumbled under his breath something about stubborn women who had to prove they were still tougher than nails.

She didn't have to prove a damn thing. Her backbone was made of steel, and just because she was old didn't mean that it was rusting. "Just do as I ask."

Pulling out his cell phone, he shook his head and sighed as Madelyn whistled for the dogs. They followed her to the three-wheeler.

She set the rifle carefully inside before turning the vehicle around. As she passed Martin, she overheard him speaking to Joe, their caretaker. Of course her son would call Joe for the job. Joe took care of everything. God help her if Joe ever decided to up and leave. The plantation she and her dead husband had built would turn to rubble within five years if he did.

Madelyn drove on the makeshift road, bouncing every now and then from the ruts the rain runoff caused. After parking, she hopped out just in time to catch Joe coming out of the garage—most likely on his way to take care of the boar.

He started toward her.

"I appreciate your helping Martin," she said when he stopped a foot away.

Her son was such a disappointment at times. Didn't matter that she was partially to blame by caving in to her dead husband's habit of spoiling their oldest boy. From the moment he took his first step, Martin had been groomed to take over Duval Incorporated. He did a bang-up job with the company, but when it came to the Duval lands, he'd just as soon let the developers have it. He preferred living in Mount Pleasant where, according to him, it was more civilized.

Civilized meant overly populated to Madelyn's way of thinking. The Charleston area wasn't huge by any means—consisting of roughly three-quarters of a million people. Yet, ever since they built the Mark Clark Expressway in 1989 and the Arthur Ravenel Junior Bridge in 2005, urban sprawl had left its mark. Madelyn thrived on open space. Living along the marshes on Johns Island suited her just fine.

"We both know Martin hates getting his hands dirty," Joe said, pulling her thoughts back to him. He smiled. "Besides, it's my pleasure, ma'am."

"Stop calling me ma'am." She frowned. "Otherwise I'll feel old."

"May I remind you that you're a year older than me, and I consider myself old."

"Reminding women of their age is rude, especially when men age much more gracefully than women."

Joe snorted. "You haven't aged a bit since I met you, twenty years ago."

Rather than argue with him, she bent to rub behind Rock's ear. Roll, clearly not wanting to miss out on the affection, nudged her other hand.

She laughed. "Good thing I have two hands." Tired of rubbing the dogs' heads, she stood and brushed her hands on her jeans.

"Have you heard anything from Lacey?"

Madelyn shook her head. "I was going to give her a call once I got back from killing the boar."

"Humph. Let me know how she's doing. If I call her, she'll think I'm checking up on her."

"I will." She smiled warmly in an effort to offset the hint of disapproval in his tone.

Joe hadn't liked the idea of his only grandchild chasing after Cade, her grandson. Even if it was for a good cause.

"If you'll excuse me, I have a bit of work ahead of me." He touched his hat in a silent salute as she nodded. Then he turned and walked toward his own three-wheeler without looking back.

Madelyn stayed glued to the spot, watching the dust kick up behind the vehicle as he sped toward Martin and the boar.

Stubborn man, she thought, wishing he could see how well suited they were for each other. But Joe had made it perfectly clear, his relationship with her would be that of an employee. He respected her dead husband's memory too much to consider wooing Madelyn. Unfortunately, Joe wasn't about to change his ways, no matter how often she pointed out that Martin Senior had been dead for more than fifteen years.

Well, she couldn't do a damn thing about that, but she was hell-bent on making sure her favorite grandchild was home for Christmas. She was tired of the wall that had been built between her oldest son and her oldest grandson.

Cade had always loved the land but he'd left it in anger, swearing never to return. And in all these years, he'd kept to those words. If Madelyn wanted to see him, she had to make the trip to Atlanta.

Once inside her spacious house, she started up the stairs on the left side where her bedroom suite took up the majority of the space. The staircase on the right went to the same place, the second floor, and led to several spacious guest suites on the opposite end. Madelyn loved having guests, but she also craved her alone time.

Shutting her bedroom door behind her to ensure privacy, she strode toward her bed and sat on the edge to tug off the hunting boots she'd worn.

She wiggled her toes, then plumped up the pillows against the ornate dark wood headboard, and grabbed her cell phone. Her gaze landed on a picture of Cade and Martin, taken in happier times before Cade's mom had died.

Joe might not like the idea of her using his granddaughter as a pawn in her plans, but Madelyn had her back to the wall. Soon after her husband's death, she'd willed the plantation to Cade, and now she worried that he'd hold on to his stupid grudge and sell it to Martin, who'd chop it into subdivisions.

After punching in Lacey's number, she leaned back and stretched out her stocking-clad feet. Madelyn had to at least try to get Cade back on Duval soil before she died in order to rekindle his love for the plantation. Otherwise, she'd have no choice but to leave it to the state as a preserve.

"Have you seen Cade?" she asked when Lacey came on the line. Ignoring the twinge of guilt that nipped at her conscience, she added, "How goes our plan?"

Having no siblings, Cade had always viewed Lacey as a younger sister. The two had grown up together. Lacey was the only person who could persuade him to come home for a visit, ensuring the Christmas miracle Madelyn longed for—to have her entire family together again.

Chapter 2

Shivering, Lacey Barnes rubbed her arms while pacing outside the coffee shop. Her light jacket did nothing to keep out the biting wind. Atlanta was much colder in early December than what she was used to.

She checked her watch, mentally debating whether to enter. He was late making his daily coffee stop, and she needed to make their meeting look like a chance encounter.

As she turned to retrace her steps, she nearly collided with a man carrying a cup of coffee. The lid flew off and half the contents splashed onto the front of Lacey's too thin coat.

"I'm terribly sorry," the man said, who'd clearly been more interested in reading his texts than watching where he was going.

"Don't worry about it," Lacey said in a begrudging voice. It wouldn't have happened if she hadn't done an about-face. Now she had no choice but to go inside, if only to keep warm. At least the coffee didn't have cream in it.

"Lacey? Is that you?"

She spun around and came face-to-face with *him*. "Cade. What a surprise."

And it truly was. If he'd been on time, her jacket wouldn't be saturated. The scent of coffee rose and her confidence dwindled. This *so* wasn't how she'd planned their reunion. God help her if he ever figured out this *unexpected* bumping into each other was intentional on her part.

Cade had always hated being manipulated—hence his exodus from Charleston. Secretly stalking him to create a spontaneous meeting amounted to as much. If she were a guy, she'd probably be arrested. Or maybe she would be, anyway. Yet considering Cade's friendly smile, she doubted he would press charges unless he discovered her sneakiness.

5

"Wow, you look great." His gorgeous blue eyes flashed male appreciation, something else that took Lacey by surprise, considering a middle full of French roast. He grabbed her hands and held them up. "You're all grown up. I almost didn't recognize you."

Subduing an urge to giggle, she couldn't help but return a similar glance. After all, this was Cade Duval, the man she compared all others to, and came up lacking.

He hadn't changed one bit; in fact, he'd grown more handsome. His brown hair was neatly trimmed. The day's growth of whiskers currently popular with guys gave him a devil-may-care look. The leather jacket he wore added to the rugged persona and didn't disguise his well-developed six-foot frame one bit. He obviously still worked out.

"It's been a while," she said, struggling to keep her eyes from revealing her attraction. Her long-lasting deep love for him was an added benefit, and probably played a bigger part in why she'd agreed to make the drive to Atlanta than she wanted to admit.

"Why don't I buy you a cup and we can catch up. Do you have a few minutes?"

Did she have a few minutes? Heavens, she'd give him a lifetime if he'd take it. Fat chance of that happening, especially once she laid her cards on the table. For now, it was better to keep them close to her drenched chest.

Swallowing the lump of guilt that caught in her throat, she nodded. If only she didn't have an agenda. His genuine joy over seeing her was a tall glass of cool water to her dehydrated love life. And she'd been thirsty since he left Charleston ten long years ago.

Warmth hit her as she stepped through the door he held open. At least inside, her jacket would dry.

She followed him up to the counter. At his questioning glance, she said, "I'll have a large coffee."

After retrieving their drinks, they moved to an empty table near the window. Cade, being the gentleman she remembered, held a chair out for her.

"Thanks," she murmured and busied herself taking off her jacket. She placed it on the chair, thankful the coffee stain hadn't spread to her blouse. With his help, she sat.

As he grabbed the chair across from her, she took a sip of coffee to avoid eye contact. Cade would surely glimpse the guilt that lurked in her gaze, and that would raise too many questions.

"What brings you to Atlanta?"

"I'm thinking of moving here," she lied. Smiling, she focused on her cup, using it to warm her hands.

"Really?" His eyes grew wide, as if her statement shocked him. "I remember you saying Charleston was the best city in the world, and that you'd never leave it."

Smoothing the paper napkin in front of her, Lacey shrugged. "When reality hits and jobs are scarce, concessions become necessary." At least there was some truth in that comment. "Charleston is a great spot for bohemians with money, but not so much for high-school grads like me with only one year of community college under her belt."

She prayed he wouldn't realize her smile was fake. "Waiting tables gets old." Another truth. "According to a customer, I was disrespectful. Rather than fight the accusation, I walked out."

Most of the upscale restaurant's customers treated the wait staff shoddily. Lacey couldn't figure out why, when it was one of dozens in the downtown market area. Still, she'd had enough *training* and felt ready to take the next step in her long-term goal.

Thankfully, Lacey had landed a job as a gopher for a wedding consultant, but that didn't start until the first week in January.

The thought of going back to waitressing in the interim was depressing, which was why Lacey ever considered doing Madelyn Duval's bidding in the first place. Get the matriarch's prodigal grandson to return to Duval Plantation for Christmas, and Lacey could start the event-planning business she'd dreamed of five years early.

The idea of pushing up her timetable had been a nice incentive, but after thinking it over, Lacey had decided she could never perpetrate such a farce and told Ms. Maddie so. The old biddy then threatened to fire Lacey's grandfather a year before his stock options in Duval Incorporated vested. Her grandfather, who'd spent the last twenty years of his life working as the Duval caretaker, would be out of the funds he'd planned to use for retirement. He would also be kicked out of the apartment over the Duval garage. In order to save the needed money for her dream, Lacey lived there with him. And Ms. Maddie, the witch, knew Lacey would be more concerned for her grandfather's fate than her own.

It was common knowledge among the Duvals that Cade thought of Lacey as one of his sisters, and Ms. Maddie had even had the gall to insist that Lacey use that to her advantage. Of course, if Madelyn Duval ever caught wind of Lacey's true feelings for Cade, she would put the brakes on the "bringing-back-Cade-before-Christmas miracle," as Lacey had coined it, in a heartbeat.

Rather than reveal her thoughts, she spread out her hands. "So here I am, looking for work and searching for the perfect apartment at the same time. Unfortunately, December isn't the best time for either." Steering the conversation toward him to avoid having to come up with more lies, she asked, "What about you? What have you been doing since you left Charleston?"

"I've started an Internet business. I peddle sunglasses and accessories." He smiled—the one that always hit her right in the heart and made her feel like she was the only one in the room—and continued talking about the company. "I have several brick-and-mortar stores in the Atlanta area. If the company maintains its current sales trajectory, I hope to expand into other states."

Considering his enthusiasm, he was proud of his accomplishments. *Deservedly so*, she thought as his voice trailed off.

"Now that I've bored you to death with all my news, tell me where you're staying."

Lacey had really hoped to avoid discussing her accommodations, but since she was getting good at twisting the truth, she said, "I have a hotel room." Basically, it was a room with a bed at a youth hostel. She shared a bath.

"A few blocks from here." Another small fib. The youth hostel was downtown, several miles from the Buckhead neighborhood.

"At least until I get settled, or more importantly, land a job." Thank God that much was true, at least for the duration of her stay.

Smiling, she risked a glance in his direction. Wrong thing to do. His warm smile, complete with crinkles around the eyes, affected her too much.

"No friend of mine is going to stay in a hotel when I have plenty of room. You can stay with me until you find an apartment."

"I couldn't." Lacey shook her head. He was just being nice.

"You can. Besides, I'll be insulted if you don't."

Her cheeks burned as her jaw dropped open for a second. "You haven't seen me in almost a decade."

"Are you telling me you've turned into an ax murderer?"

She laughed. "No."

"A cat burglar?"

"No," she said. But she wasn't being totally honest, either.

Still, living with him would make her job easier by giving her more access to him in the next few weeks. In the meantime, she'd have to figure out some way to get him to go home with her for Christmas.

Easy-peasy? Right?

Heavens no, she told herself, staring into his sexy blue eyes. No man should be that attractive. Of course, having glanced around the room, she noted ten other men who were just as attractive. So why did she have to be fixated on him?

"Cade?"

Lacey turned toward the voice as a gorgeous blonde walked up to the table, giving Cade a possessive glance.

Cade stood and kissed the newcomer on the lips before turning back to her. "Lacey Barnes, this is Brandy Vincent."

Cade has a girlfriend? Of course someone like him would. She should have expected it.

Quickly recovering from the initial shock and struggling to hide her dismay, Lacey stood and held out her hand. "Nice to meet you."

Brandy ignored the gesture as her assessing gaze took a trip over Lacey. "Likewise, I'm sure," she said in a voice that said the opposite.

Noting Brandy's manicured nails, Lacey nonchalantly lowered her arm. In an attempt to hide fingernails that were chipped and unpolished, she returned to her seat and clasped her hands on her lap.

Normally, women like Brandy didn't bother Lacey. She'd always joked about lacking the gene that gave most females the desire to shop or the need for manicures. Lacey never followed fashion trends.

She preferred the classic look, which never went out of style. And those few manicures she'd had for her friends' weddings never lasted long because Lacey always had her hands in stuff, whether it be dirt, water, or paint.

"Would you like something?" Cade asked Brandy.

"Thank you, darling. I'll have my usual."

As soon as Cade was out of earshot, Brandy looked down her nose at Lacey. "So you're a friend of Cade's?" Considering her enunciation of the word *friend*, she obviously didn't believe it.

"Yes. My grandfather works for his grandmother," was all Lacey could get out.

The ensuing silence was torturous.

Lacey struggled not to fidget. Being this close to someone who was dressed to kill, one who obviously had a professional makeup artist and hairstylist at her beck and call, left Lacey feeling even more plain and unattractive. Worse, she couldn't think of a single thing to say that would change the description.

Thankfully, Cade strode back up to the table and set Brandy's frou-frou drink in front of her.

Another glaring difference. Lacey preferred coffee. Her only splurge was adding cream, which just added more weight to the plainness that permeated her consciousness.

"So, darling, I'm going to have to cancel our dinner date tonight."

Cade frowned. "That's two in a row."

One of those perfectly manicured hands reached for his and stroked it as Brandy practically purred, "We'll have plenty of time to make up for it once these modeling jobs are out of the way. I promise." She then went on to explain how tedious they were, but as she spoke, she didn't once glance at Lacey.

Having endured enough of Brandy's cold shoulder, Lacey stood. "Well. If you'll excuse me, I have an interview I have to get to. It was nice meeting you, Brandy." Without waiting for a reply that wouldn't come, she turned to Cade and offered him a genuine smile. "And I enjoyed catching up."

Lacey grabbed her jacket, hoping it was dry. But it didn't matter. She couldn't get out of there fast enough.

It was obvious Brandy and Cade were tight. Were they lovers? Oh God. Lacey mentally groaned and wished she hadn't come. Somehow, some way, she'd have to repay the money she'd already spent. The thought of letting her grandfather down entered her consciousness, but she didn't see how she could remedy the situation when it meant watching Cade hook up with another woman. She'd endured enough of that as a teen.

As she darted for the exit, Cade said, "Wait."

Lacey felt his hand on her elbow at the same time the one word hit her ears. She halted and spun around. Glancing into his apologetic gaze was a huge mistake.

She looked away. "I'm fine, Cade. Really I am."

"I meant it when I invited you to stay with me."

"What about your girlfriend?"

"I'm sure she'll understand."

Lacey wasn't so sure, but she refrained from saying so.

"Besides," Cade added, "my place is huge, and I'd appreciate the company. No strings. Here, give me your phone number, and I'll text you the address and tell you where the spare key is hidden."

Lacey mentally debated the pros and cons for a few seconds. It was probably a big mistake to give in, but she couldn't say no. As she rattled off her number, a realization set in. When it came to Cade Duval, she had a masochistic side to rival Leopold Masoch's, the man who first coined the term.

When done typing, Cade stuck the phone back in his pocket.

"Thanks." She was about to turn around, but his hands on her shoulders stopped her.

He pulled her in for a hug, and no power on earth could keep her from returning it. This was what she'd craved for ten long years. She stepped back when she caught Brandy's glare over Cade's shoulder.

"I guess I'll see you later," she said, offering him a wobbly smile.

As she walked away, she prayed she could survive her task. Or more importantly, survive once Cade was back in the Duval fold with Brandy by his side.

But then again, maybe Lacey's journey would bring an end to her obsession with the man, so she could have what she'd always wanted. A family of her own.

One could only hope.

Chapter 3

Cade watched Lacey until she was out of sight before returning to the table where Brandy waited. Impatiently, judging by the way those long blood-red nails drummed on the table in quick staccato taps.

Brandy was a stunner, no doubt about it, but when she pouted, like now, it camouflaged some of that beauty. In fact, over the course of the past ten minutes, Cade had begun to find it downright ugly, especially when compared to Lacey's sunny girl-next-door disposition. He couldn't remember Lacey ever pouting.

"So, who was that?" Her tone did nothing to improve on his opinion.

"I told you. A friend from home."

"Really? A friend?" Her brows arched and her eyes flashed disbelief. "She must've been a *good* friend the way you hugged her good-bye."

"I grew up with her, so yeah, she is. But you have no reason to be jealous, Brandy." It irked him that he even had to say it out loud.

Mollified, Brandy relaxed and started telling him about her news.

As she droned on and on about the photo shoot she'd nailed for this weekend, his mind wandered to his chance meeting with Lacey. He found he rather liked the idea of showing her *his* Atlanta.

"My agent landed me another job but it's a beach shoot in Florida, which means I'll be gone for a couple of weeks." She snapped her fingers in front of his face when he didn't respond properly. "Hello! Earth to Cade! Are you there?"

"I'm listening." Damn. The woman had radar that homed in whenever she wasn't the center of attention. "Two weeks, huh?" He shook his head and offered a *that's too bad* expression. "When do you leave?"

"Six a.m. Monday morning. Which only gives us Friday night. It will have to be an early one, though, and I can't spend the night since I need my beauty sleep."

Cade grunted, still going for a disappointed mien when in reality, he was relieved. At least he wouldn't have to explain why Lacey was staying with him. A twinge of guilt pricked his conscience for keeping quiet about having Lacey as a houseguest, and he couldn't figure out why when Lacey was like a kid sister to him.

You know why, his conscience shouted.

Okay, he mentally conceded.

Why argue with himself when he couldn't dismiss the spark of attraction that flared into a momentary lustful thought when he'd first spied Lacey. Nor could he deny he'd enjoyed talking to her. Or that his gut had contracted when she'd smiled.

Still, it wasn't as if he was some horny teenager. He could easily handle being with Lacey. All grown up and—

Brandy's brittle laugh filled the air.

Cade smiled, having no idea of what she'd just said. Concentrating on Brandy right now took way too much effort, especially since she was talking about herself, as usual, and he couldn't shake thoughts of Lacey. In his defense, any man who was still breathing would find his childhood friend appealing. The girl he'd known all his life, and thought of as a little sister, had filled out in all the right places.

Besides, he could be himself with her. The ridiculous notion stopped him cold.

Brandy was part of the world of fashion, which he loved. But thinking about their relationship now made him realize that he pretty much let her make all their plans. For the life of him, he had no idea how it had happened. Hell, if he'd wanted to be micromanaged, he'd have stayed in Charleston and gone to work for his overbearing dad. Obviously, Brandy being gone so much had to have something to do with it.

It was definitely time to set down some ground rules. Once Brandy returned from her modeling stint. In the meantime, what harm could come of enjoying a few weeks with someone he didn't have to impress? Lacey knew all of his faults and he knew all of hers.

When Cade realized that he couldn't wait until he got home tonight, it should have concerned him. That it didn't should have concerned him more.

But it didn't.

Chapter 4

Noting Madelyn Duval's name on the small screen, Lacey sighed. Ms. Maddie, the nosiest woman on the planet, most likely wanted another update. Lacey probably shouldn't have let it slip about her planned encounter that morning.

"Hi, Ms. Maddie," she said after answering.

As expected, the older woman wanted to know how things were going.

"I've seen Cade. And *your* plan is right on schedule. Everything is just fine."

Glancing back at the big, imposing house, Lacey spoke in an upbeat tone, but deep down she wasn't fine. Not even close. She'd parked in front of what looked to be a mansion just moments ago, after double-checking the address and Google Maps. This exclusive neighborhood off Highway 41 and Arden Road NW wasn't what she expected. But she should have. After all, his family was worth billions.

"As a matter of fact, I'm staying with Cade. He wouldn't accept anything else."

"Of course not. He's a Duval," Madelyn shot back in a pleased voice. "He knows how to treat friends he considers family."

Lacey nodded. Yep, she was just a good friend. What's more, she should get used to the idea. This house and the apartment she shared with her grandfather were light-years apart. Dreaming for more was aiming for a galaxy far, far away. It wasn't going to happen in her lifetime.

"I'm a little early." She glanced at her watch. "He should be here any minute."

At least, that's what his text had stated, along with instructions on where to find the key, in case he got behind at work. Once he arrived, she'd have to start working on getting Cade to see the wisdom of returning home for Christmas this year.

"I hope you're prepared for the worst," Lacey said, also reminding Ms. Maddie that he'd already missed the last nine Christmases, Thanksgivings, and other holidays.

"I have faith in you. After all, you're Joe's granddaughter."

Despite Ms. Maddie's confident tone, Lacey wasn't so sure, mainly having no idea of how to go about the arduous task. *Fake it.* That was the main crux of her plan.

A sporty black Jaguar pulled into his driveway, drawing her attention. Lacey recognized Cade as the driver.

"I gotta run. He just got here," she said, quelling the flapping butterflies that suddenly took up residence in her tummy.

She took a deep breath as Ms. Maddie said, "Then I'll let you go, but I expect a full report on how our plan is going later tonight."

"Our plan? Don't you mean *your* plan?" Lacey grumbled under her breath as she disconnected the call.

She stuffed the phone into her purse. About to reach for the door handle, she looked up to see that Cade had made his way to her car and was already ahead of her.

"I see you found the place."

Cade took a step back, opened the door all the way, and reached for her arm to help her climb out of her tiny blue Kia Rio, a mere stepchild to the sleek car in front of it. Another reminder of their different worlds. A model like Brandy would expect Jags and big houses. Things—mostly expensive things like those—made Lacey feel uncomfortable and foolish. Plus, it seemed like a big waste of resources to a minimalist like her.

Now out of the car, Lacey tried to ignore the tingling in her arm from Cade's touch. When he finally let go of her arm, she felt a sense of loss. Not wanting to dwell on it, she did a full circle, taking in the surroundings, which appeared lush, even without leaves on the trees. Her gaze went to the house for a long second before settling on Cade.

"Wow, you weren't kidding. You really do have a lot of room."

Cade shrugged and grabbed her hand. "I'm renovating it. I'm more than halfway done. When it's finished, I'll sell it for a tidy profit and move on to the next fixer-upper."

"Fixer-upper?" She laughed. Apparently rich people had different ideas about what the word meant. No fixer-upper she'd ever seen looked like that.

"Come on. I'll show you what I've done." The tingling was back as he gave a slight tug to her hand and started walking. "We can get your bags later."

With no choice but to follow, she did. The entire time she walked beside him, heat streaked up her arm from his touch.

"So you flip houses?" she asked, steering her thoughts in another direction.

"Yep. It's how I was able to finance my business. That and what I inherited from my mom when she died. Without enough capital for start-up costs, a new business is more likely to fail."

Lacey totally understood that concept. It was why she strived to put every cent she could into savings.

"I didn't want to find venture capital and have partners, so I spent the first five years buying fixer-uppers, renovating them, and then selling for a profit."

"Wait a minute. I'm confused. Aren't renovations a big part of Duval Incorporated, so in essence, isn't that what your dad's company does?"

Duval Incorporated also bought dilapidated property, demolished existing structures, and created mega-buildings, along with developing untouched land into mega-communities.

"Yeah. But this is my company, and I don't have Dad micromanaging me."

Since he brought up his father, she felt safe asking, "Have you talked to him lately?"

"I called him and Grandmother on Thanksgiving. It was a strained conversation, just like the one I had with him on his birthday."

"I can't believe you haven't been back to Charleston in all these years." At least the statement provided her a foundation on which to build.

"It's easier if I stay away."

She offered him a woeful smile. "That's so sad."

"That's life in my family."

"Have you ever thought about going back?" She eyed him expectantly. Crossing the fingers of the hand behind her back that Cade wasn't holding on to, she went for broke. "Like, say, for Christmas?"

A shrug was his only answer, which didn't tell her much. Was he shrugging off the idea entirely, or was he open to the suggestion? Time would hopefully tell.

By now they'd made it to the porch, but veranda was a better description. Cade moved to open the front door, a beautifully ornate one with elaborate stained glass and wood. The door alone probably cost more than her car.

Inside, the modern stone flooring and white woodwork in the foyer blended with the more traditional curved staircase and two-story chandelier.

"It's breathtaking." Awestruck, she did a three-sixty.

"You should have seen it when I bought it. I've completely renovated the first floor. The upstairs is about half done. Would you like a tour?"

"Are you kidding? I'd love one."

"Follow me."

He led her toward the kitchen that opened to a great room. Wall-to-wall windows revealed a view of a patio, a pool, and what looked to be a mini forest beyond.

"The appliances are state of the art."

"I love the granite countertops." She ran a hand over the smooth finish, cool to the touch. If ever she was able to buy a house, that would be one of her splurges. Didn't matter that it was ostentatious, expensive, and unnecessary. Lacey loved the look of it.

The other restored rooms on the first floor were just as gorgeous as the kitchen and great room. As they headed upstairs, several steps creaked underneath their feet.

"I need to fix that before I sell."

"Oh, I don't know. I kind of like the squeaks. It gives the house character."

Cade tsk-tsked. "A buyer spending millions for a home expects perfection."

Lacey glanced down at the recently refinished wooden stairs, noting that, as with everything else she'd seen thus far, they appeared pretty perfect to her. So what if they made a little noise? Just another difference to add to her list of reasons why she and Cade would never be on the same planet.

She discarded the thought and followed him into the master suite, tastefully decorated with traditional furnishings.

Suite definitely fit the title. Lacey couldn't call it anything other than that when she could put the apartment she shared with her grandfather in the bathroom alone. It would take more than a little adjusting to get used to luxury like this.

When her glance hit the four-poster king-sized bed, she remembered Cade's girlfriend. How often did Brandy share Cade's bed?

Suddenly, her good mood vanished. Lacey didn't want to think of Cade making love to anyone but her. Obviously, that wasn't even a slight possibility, so she remained silent as he led her down the hallway.

Cade stopped at a closed door. "This is my guest room." He pushed the door open, then stepped aside. "It's the only other room I've finished restoring up here."

Upon entering, Lacey noted another spacious room done in inviting colors, yellows and blues. One wall had a huge picture window overlooking the grounds that were now more brown than green. But in the summertime, Lacey was sure the view would be a treat to wake up to. Catty-corner to that wall was a door that led to a full bathroom with walk-in shower.

"That's it for the tour." Cade stuck his hands in his back pockets and leaned against the door frame. After a long pause, he stood up straight and cleared his throat. "Make yourself comfortable, and I'll go and get your bags out of your car."

Lacey smiled. "Thanks. It's unlocked."

Why bother locking it when no one would bother it in this neighborhood, other than to tow it away. Since it was in the driveway and out of sight of the street, that didn't seem likely.

When he was gone, Lacey walked over to the window and looked out. The sun was low on the horizon. Full darkness would soon set in. Prevalent shadows and a slight breeze were changing the shapes of the trees as she continued staring. Lacey rubbed her arms, wondering at the craziness of being in Cade's house, sleeping just doors away from him.

For the hundredth time since Cade had invited her, she berated herself for accepting his invitation.

"Here you go."

She jumped at Cade's voice and turned to see him enter the room, lugging her two bags as if they weighed nothing.

He dropped them in front of what looked to be a closet. "You pack light for someone who's moving to a new town."

"I only brought essentials. Most of my stuff is in boxes. I thought I'd wait until I had an actual apartment to live in before I had Grandpa ship my things."

Heavens, if anyone had suggested a month ago that she'd be able to lie so well, she'd have told them they were nuts. Apparently, she was a natural. The realization didn't set all that well inside her tummy.

Cade nodded, then headed for the hallway. "I need to do a few things for work. Give me about an hour. After that I'll cook dinner."

"Wow. You're actually cooking for me?"

He stopped and spun around. Capturing her gaze, he smiled— the one that grabbed her insides and twisted them into a tight knot.

"Of course."

Lacey tossed out a quick laugh. "A girl could get used to such luxury, you know. I hope Brandy realizes what a gem she has in you." Jeez, why not shout it out that she was jealous?

Instead of responding, Cade just resumed his exit, saying over his shoulder, "I hope you like steak."

"I do," she shouted after him, adding under her breath, "I'd like anything you cooked."

As the door clicked shut behind him, a sense of isolation mixed with loneliness settled over Lacey's shoulders. She missed her grandfather and the plantation. There was always something going on around Ms. Maddie. No one who met the lady actually believed her age, thinking her decades younger because she worked side by side with Lacey's grandfather, ignoring Joe's comments about letting the paid help do what they were paid to do.

Lacey sighed and set about unpacking. The sooner she persuaded Cade to make it home for Christmas, the sooner her life could get back to normal.

Unfortunately, after seeing him again, she doubted her life would ever be normal. Worse, this time around, it would take ten times longer to get him out of her system. What she'd always considered a wild teenage crush, was more.

A whole lot more.

Chapter 5

"**M**mm. That smells good."

Cade let go of the oven door as he spun around to face Lacey. In a heartbeat, his mood soared. There was something clean and fresh about Lacey, he thought, watching her walk toward him. She'd changed into sweats and was wearing slippers.

"I see you're making yourself at home."

"I hope you don't mind. I'm still getting used to the cooler temperatures."

"Not at all."

He rather liked the idea of her feeling comfortable enough to dress down. First thing he usually did when he arrived home from a day at the office was to change into jeans or sweats, if he happened to be wearing a suit. He preferred dressing casually as often as possible, much to Brandy's disapproval. It was one of the few things he'd remained firm about during the few months they'd dated. That woman would get all gussied up just to eat in front of the TV. Of course, they seldom did that, so it never was a big issue.

"I can turn up the heat."

"I'm fine." She glanced around. "Is there anything I can do?"

"Nope. Everything's just about done." He nodded to the two bottles of opened wine on the counter. "I'm having a glass of wine. Would you like one?"

"Sounds nice."

Her smile could light up the dark December night outside, it was so bright and sunny. It was warm too. It certainly warmed his heart and made him realize he'd missed her more than he ever thought possible these past ten years. The two of them used to be the best of friends, and yet he hadn't even had the decency to keep in touch with her. Since she was here now, he hoped to make it up to her with hospitality. It was the least he could do.

Reaching for a wineglass, he looked at her with eyebrows lifted. "Red or white?"

"I prefer white."

He poured, handed her the glass, and then went back to his dinner, glad that he'd had the foresight to give his housekeeper the rest of the day off. As he emptied the boiling water before mashing the potatoes, he felt Lacey watching him. The idea warmed him even more and added to his sense of well-being. He hadn't been this relaxed in a long while, he realized, setting the pot back on the stove and adding butter and milk.

Neither spoke as he whipped.

"I feel kind of useless just watching you slave away," she finally said, breaking the silence between them. "Can I at least set the table?"

"Have at it." He opened the silverware drawer, then continued whipping his potatoes. "I thought all women liked being waited on."

"Takes some getting used to, I guess. Just like the house."

"Now I feel insulted. I thought you liked me and my house."

His tone was much more suggestive than he'd meant. The words just slipped out of their own volition. Jeez, why not scare her away on her first night?

"Sorry," he murmured. "I keep forgetting we haven't seen each other in a long time." Back on Johns Island, they'd kidded around like that all the time, but that was ten years ago. A lot had changed since then.

She laughed. "Don't be. I knew you were just kidding." Bumping his hip like she used to do, she pushed past him and began riffling through the drawer, pulling out knives, forks, and spoons.

Then, as if they'd done it every day of her life, Lacey proceeded to set the table while he went back to whipping potatoes.

When done, Cade spooned them into a serving bowl, doing the same to the asparagus that he'd sautéed. The oven timer buzzed and he took out the broiled steaks.

"I like my steaks rare, but I settled on medium rare tonight, since it seemed like a safe choice. If that's too rare for you, I can always put it back in for a few minutes."

"Medium rare is perfect," she said, having obviously finished her task.

After spearing each steak and placing both on a platter, he handed it to her. "I marinated these for a few days, so cutting through them will be like slicing through butter."

Then he picked up the asparagus and potatoes, and together they walked toward the dining room table, where he set the dishes down before relieving her of the steaks and doing the same.

"It looks wonderful," she said.

He moved to turn the lights in the great room way down. Earlier he'd lit candles, and now their glow in the center of the table was romantic.

Had that been an intentional move on his part? Nah. He just liked the ambience of eating by candlelight. Besides, there was enough light spilling from the kitchen area that made things appear more normal.

As he helped Lacey into the chair she stood behind, her stomach gurgled loud enough for him to hear.

"Oops," she said, sitting and covering her mouth with a hand. She smothered a giggle and picked up her glass of wine. After taking a sip, she said, "I didn't realize how hungry I am."

He sat and reached for the platter that held the steaks. "Words every cook likes to hear."

Silently, they passed the dishes back and forth and then began to eat.

Surreptitiously, Cade watched Lacey cut off a piece of meat and place a bite into her mouth.

She closed her eyes as if experiencing pure bliss. "This steak is to die for."

A twinge of heat shot toward his groin at the thought of Lacey wearing that same satisfied expression after a night of lovemaking with him.

Cade squelched the thought and said, "At least my efforts haven't been in vain."

She threw him a puzzled look. "Why would you say that?"

"Brandy isn't into eating my cooking." He shrugged, remembering the one and only time he'd cooked for her. She'd nibbled on the vegetables without even touching the main course. "I spent hours making seafood crepes, and she complained that eating something with all that butter and cream would make her fat."

"She is a model," Lacey said, as if that explained it perfectly, which it did.

"Yeah, but sometimes it gets old. She snubbed my favorite meal for the rice cakes she pulled out of the big bag she always carries. The memory still irks me."

"You'll never catch me eating rice cakes," Lacey said, laughing. She took another bite, and added after swallowing it, "I exercise regularly in an attempt to keep my weight down, but if given a choice between eating good food and gaining a few ounces, I'll always eat first, then worry later."

He gave her a once-over before letting his gaze land on hers. "You don't look like you have anything to worry about."

In fact, she had curves in all the right places. Curves that were sharp angles on Brandy. Cade was beginning to realize he liked curves better than sharp angles. He certainly liked Lacey's curves.

Don't even go there, his conscience warned.

Heeding the warning, he turned the conversation to something he'd been curious about since first spying her outside the Starbucks that morning.

"Since we've moved on to current loves and their failings, tell me. Whatever happened to Jonathan?" he asked of her high-school sweetheart. Ten years ago, she was really into him.

Lacey took a drink of wine, rolling the liquid around in her mouth, appearing as if she were mulling over her next words. "We broke up. About a year after you left town."

"Oh? That's too bad." He shook his head and sobered when he realized he was actually smiling. The news shouldn't have pleased him that much, but it did. Go figure. "I thought for sure you two would get married."

She started laughing.

"What's so funny?"

"Nothing." Her smile died, and suddenly the laughter went out of her eyes. "It's pretty sad, actually." She lifted her glass. "Here's to finding out he was gay and not wasting any more time with him than I already had."

Cade almost spit out the steak he was chewing. "Excuse me?" he said, once he could speak. He looked at her dumbfounded. "Are you telling me Jonathan was gay?"

Her face a frozen mask, she stared straight ahead and nodded. "I found out when I thought we'd make love after our senior prom. But that was before I realized he had the hots for Reggie and was only using me to make him jealous. It obviously worked, because I caught them kissing behind the bleachers that night."

He whistled through his teeth. "That beats my worst dating story."

"I see it as a blessing in disguise. Thankfully, I found out before I made more of a fool of myself. He acted as if I should have known. Apparently, he also was dating me to keep his parents from finding out."

"Lacey, I'm really sorry."

"So am I. But it's all in the past." She glanced at him with those saucer-big eyes that said *it might be past history, but it still hurt.*

For some reason Cade couldn't fathom, he wanted to ease the pain that that bozo had obviously caused her. Plus, he felt guilty for not being there for her.

Hell, she'd been there for him when Patty Sue had dumped him at the beginning of his sophomore year in high school. The very night it had happened, he'd gotten drunk and had gone down to the marsh, but Lacey had showed up out of the blue and had commenced cheering him up. After talking with her for less than an hour, he'd felt renewed and less like someone's doormat—which was what he'd been before Patty Sue dumped him for another guy.

In fact, the main reason she dumped him was because he wouldn't go to church with her. Not that he was against church, it just wasn't his church, and she got all pissy about his refusal. Still, Patty Sue knew how to use her tongue. She'd been his first, but he hadn't been hers.

Months later, after he caught wind that her current guy was no better than a puppy dog, doing anything and everything to please her, he realized that he'd dodged a bullet with her. Last he heard, they were married and her husband was the lapdog she'd needed, the one that Cade could never be. Thanks to Lacey, he'd gotten over her sooner, rather than later.

"Are you seeing anyone now?" Why he asked, he wasn't sure. He just knew he had to have the answer.

"No."

That answer shouldn't have pleased him as much as it did. He dug into his meal with a little more gusto.

As they ate, they talked. During that hour, Cade was taken back in time. He hadn't been this open with anyone since he'd left home all those years ago, and he said as much to Lacey.

"Why do people always remember the bad things that happen, rather than the good?" That was something worth pondering. For later. "Looking back, I'd forgotten about all the good times. What I remember most is feeling hemmed in, unable to breathe with my dad hanging over my shoulder, watching and criticizing everything I did. Which, by the way, was mainly to please him."

Cade threw out a humorless laugh before adding, "Of course, quitting the Citadel halfway through the first semester of my senior year was pretty stupid. In my defense, I couldn't take it any longer. I was tired of everyone telling me what to do. I hated the regimentation."

Cade hadn't intended to delve so deep into his feelings. Yet he felt comfortable talking to Lacey. She'd always seemed mature for her age, and he sensed she understood him. A silly thought, but it was the truth.

"According to Dad, I could never measure up to the Duval expectations. My dad is the oldest son and I'm the oldest grandkid. As such, I had more to prove." He sighed and took a long drink of wine, thankful for its mellowing effect. Somehow it didn't seem as big a burden any longer. "I always felt the pressure of being a Duval. Expectations were high, and every grandchild had made their mark in real estate and developing along with my uncles. My cousins were all successful before they even started college, but not me. I hated those summers I had to work for Dad."

Cade was always more attached to his mother, before she died. He considered himself more of a Reece than a Duval, and his dad seemed to hate that side of him. The horrible fight that drove him to Atlanta was never far from his consciousness, when his dad had called him gay. Martin had been very blunt about the fact that he thought Cade was a failure. All because Cade was interested in men's fashion.

As mellow as he was, he couldn't reveal that. It still hurt too much to think about, even after ten years. Instead he said, "My mom always said I was too creative for my own good. If she'd been alive, I'm sure I'd have been able to go to Juilliard, like I wanted. Instead, I caved and went to my dad and granddad's alma mater."

He picked up his wineglass and eyed it wistfully. Thoughts of his mother always made him sad.

"Do you still miss your mom?" Lacey asked after a long pause.

"Every day." He nodded and took a long sip. "She was the one person my dad would listen to. You know, a buffer between us." Cade gave her a considering glance. "Here I am, hogging the conversation and moaning about losing my mom, and you lost both your parents. Do you miss them?"

The fact that both of them had lost their mothers was what brought them together in the first place all those years ago, but Lacey had been left without both a mother or a father, and at a much younger age.

"I don't remember much about my dad. He wasn't around as much, and I was six when they died. I still remember my mom, though. She smelled like roses. In fact, whenever I smell roses, her smiling face comes to mind." Lacey fingered her wineglass as a soft smile lit her expression. "It's the same thing with cookies. Mom always used to bake chocolate-chip cookies. I can't pass a bakery without thinking of those days when I'd help her."

After that, their conversation came to a natural end. A few minutes later, Cade stood. Lacey jumped up and grabbed her plate.

"Leave it."

"I'll help you clean up."

He shook his head. "No need."

He reached for their wineglasses and started for the sofa a few feet away. After setting them down on the coffee table, he retrieved the two bottles of wine, white for her and red for him, from the kitchen. About to sit, he glanced back at her and noted that she was still standing at the table, eyeing him with a confused expression.

"I can't just leave it." Her no-nonsense tone added to the statement.

Concentrating on refilling the wineglasses, he said, "I have a housekeeper who comes in daily. She gets all weird if she doesn't have something to do."

"A housekeeper? Really?"

He stopped pouring and turned her way. "It's not what you think."

Why he felt a need to defend himself, he wasn't sure. But he damn sure didn't like seeing the hint of disdain in her look.

"Camila sort of came with the house. She's in her early sixties and needs the job until she can collect Social Security. No one else will hire her because of age discrimination. I've told her that as long as I own this house, she'll have a job. After that, if she still needs to work, I'll find something for her to do."

"You're a very nice man, Cade," Lacey said, moving toward him. The smile she bestowed upon him made him feel as if he'd just done something spectacular, like curing cancer, rather than figuring out a symbiotic solution to both his situation and Camila's.

Had Brandy ever looked at him like that? He couldn't remember. In fact, he couldn't remember any of his girlfriends in the recent past giving him such a warm look. Mostly it seemed as if they were with him because of what he brought to their lives, usually his net worth.

After all, most were wealthy women with lucrative jobs. Maybe that's why he found Lacey so attractive. She had no interest in what he was worth. He had a sneaking suspicion she'd prefer him if he weren't so well off. It was definitely worth thinking about.

Lacey neared the sofa. Halting, she cleared her throat.

"What now?" she asked, wrapping her arms around her middle, as if she was warding off the cold. Or maybe it was him she was warding off.

"We can watch a movie or continue talking." He patted the seat beside him, then held up the wine he'd poured. "Come on. I don't bite. Besides, it's still too early to turn in, and I'd rather have the stimulating company than be alone."

He was alone too much as it was. Funny, until he'd had dinner with Lacey, he hadn't realized exactly how lonely he was.

As she sat, being careful to leave a good foot between them, he reminded himself that she was off-limits. She was like a sister. And he had a girlfriend.

I know, I know, he told his pesky conscience, doubling up his efforts to remember both. Besides, she was already slightly wary. No sense in making her more so by doing something he'd regret tomorrow. Like kissing her as he was dying to do.

Chapter 6

Lacey woke up late the next morning. Light spilled into the room from the window. As she stretched, a sense of the world being righted on its axis filled her. Or maybe it was the gorgeous view that added to her contentment. It really was a treat to wake up to such beauty without having to get out of bed. Of course, the views of the marshes in the Lowcountry were spectacular, especially at sunset.

Unfortunately, Lacey's bedroom window at home faced the front gravel driveway of the Duval mansion. Peering out at tiny rocks wasn't nearly as nice.

A quick glance at the clock had her jumping out of bed. She'd couldn't remember a time in recent history she'd slept so late.

Lacey quickly showered and brushed her teeth. As she came out of the bathroom, there was a knock on the bedroom door. Doing up the last few buttons on her blouse, she rushed to see if maybe Cade was paying her a good-morning visit.

"Buenos dias, señorita." A rotund Hispanic woman about five feet tall entered, carrying a tray. "I brought you some breakfast. I hope you like coffee. I make a big pot. Señor Cade, he say he not sure if you drink it or not, so I make tea too. Just in case." She nodded and gave her an expectant smile. "Sí?"

Lacey returned her smile. "You must be Camila. Cade told me all about you."

"Sí. And you are Señorita Lacey." After setting the tray down on the table in front of the magnificent view, Camila pulled out one of the two chairs around it and patted the seat. "Come. You eat breakfast, okay?"

Figuring it was better to obey than argue, Lacey sat. She poured herself a cup of coffee, added a bit of cream, then propped her feet on the other chair and peered out at the beautiful morning.

A couple of squirrels running up a tree caught her attention, as did a few birds eating from a feeder in the yard. She had to admit it was nice to be served like this and to enjoy a filling breakfast of eggs and toast while taking in the idyllic scenery.

As Lacey ate, Camila busied herself in the bathroom, then returned to the bedroom and began picking up the few items Lacey had left on the floor the previous night.

When Lacey realized Camila was about to make her bed, she said, "Please, you don't have to do that."

Camila, who'd begun fluffing the pillows, stopped in mid-fluff. "Surely you are not telling me you prefer to do this yourself? Otherwise, I will not earn the generous salary Señor Cade pays me."

"Of course not. I wouldn't think of depriving you of your livelihood." Lacey bit back a smile, not wanting the feisty woman to know she found her attitude amusing and most refreshing. It was obvious the idea of not earning her keep was the worst thing possible.

Three-fourths of the waitresses and waiters Lacey had worked with over the past five years had a poor work ethic. More than half got fired for that very reason. Her grandfather claimed it was generational. But it seemed to Lacey it was more a societal issue rather than a generational one. They used to spend hours debating stuff like that.

A pang of homesickness struck. Then she remembered last night and her homesickness morphed into confidence. Her task at hand didn't seem insurmountable any longer. Cade hadn't changed one bit. Oh, he was older and probably wiser, but he was still the tenderhearted sophomore who'd had his heart broken by some stupid bimbo who didn't know his worth. Even at eleven years of age, Lacey had known.

Still, it really was too bad that Cade had distanced himself from family like he had. More memories surfaced from her evening with him, and she knew without a doubt, he *needed* to go home. Suddenly, she was glad Ms. Maddie had sent her.

Filled with a sense of urgency to get on with her plans, she finished eating and drank the rest of her coffee.

Camila, having made the bed, nodded at the tray with the empty dishes. "Done, sí?"

"Sí," Lacey said, jumping up and giving the shorter woman a hug. "I'm done."

An embarrassed tint of pink hit the maid's cheeks as she bent to pick up the tray. "I will have lunch ready at noon. That's when Señor Cade comes home to eat."

"He comes home for lunch?"

Camila's nod was her only answer as she left the room.

Awesome. Lacey did a fist pump. She couldn't wait to see him.

Down, Lacey. He has a girlfriend. She ignored the thought and rushed to the closet, intending to change. She wanted to look her best.

Hon, her subconscious shouted. *You couldn't compete with Brandy even if you had her slim figure and expensive clothes. You are a mousy-haired plain Jane, and she's a gorgeous blonde.*

The startling facts brought her up short, and just as quickly as her good mood had arrived, it vanished.

Lacey moped around the mansion, going into the unfinished rooms and trying to figure out what they would look like once Cade refurbished them.

Brandy was glamourous and fit this place. As comfortable as Lacey felt here, she also knew she was way out of her element. She didn't have a glamourous bone in her body. She was into making slipcovers and pottery, and enjoyed gardening.

Ms. Maddie actually paid her for planting rosebushes last year. Ordinarily, Lacey wouldn't have taken any money, but Ms. Maddie knew of her plans for starting her own business and wouldn't hear of not paying her the same amount the local nursery was going to charge.

With still a couple of hours to kill until Cade made it home for lunch, Lacey roamed the garden. She walked the path several times. It was a brisk late fall day. Sunlight filtered through the deciduous tree branches that had recently lost leaves.

Lacey found a sunny spot on a nearby bench and plopped down. Lifting her head to the warm rays, she closed her eyes and forced herself to relax.

Which lasted for all of five minutes.

Enough of this. Relaxing wasn't something she was good at. Lacey preferred being productive.

She jumped up, intending to go for a walk. Or better yet, call the bakery with the help-wanted sign that she'd passed by several times while waiting for Cade the day before.

Cell phone in hand, she made the call and spoke with the owner. The position for a part-time counter person was still open.

"I should warn you," Susan Hendricks said. "I only need someone for fifteen hours a week with no benefits. Seven to ten, Monday through Friday. I usually hire a high school kid on winter break, but no one has applied for that time slot yet. The one big drawback is that the job ends in January when things slow down."

"That sounds perfect for me."

Lacey would be gone in January. There wasn't a more perfect solution to her boredom, and this one just fell into her lap. Ms. Maddie didn't say anything about not earning extra money. Although twelve dollars an hour didn't amount to much.

"I can be there in twenty minutes, and I can start work immediately." Then she added, "I may have to leave before Christmas, though."

The woman paused. When the silence on the line continued, Lacey crossed her fingers and sent up a little prayer.

She exhaled a sigh of relief when the woman said, "That should work. I have someone I can call for that week. She's not available now, or I wouldn't be trying to fill the position."

Lacey hung up and ran to her room to change. In no time, she was pulling into a parking spot behind the bakery where Susan told her to park. While she was climbing out of her car, movement from the Dumpster drew her attention, and huge brown eyes that belonged to what looked to be a mutt, an ugly one at that, stared back at her.

"Shoo," a voice said from behind Lacey.

She glanced toward the back of the bakery, and the person who'd spoken was stamping her foot. The dog whimpered and scampered out of sight.

"He's obviously hungry." Lacey's attention returned to the spot where it had disappeared before refocusing on the lady.

"I'd prefer that he pester someone else for food." The attractive woman's pixie cut fit her face. No one could call her hair mousy either. Plus, that sharp brown-eyed gaze that gave Lacey a once-over could only be called thorough. "I take it you're Lacey Barnes?"

Lacey must have passed inspection, because the woman smiled and held out her hand. "I'm Susan Hendricks. Everyone just calls me Sue."

Lacey shook her hand and followed her inside. Sue gave her a quick interview, then hired her on the spot.

"Let me introduce you to Jen. She'll be training you, hopefully tomorrow." Sue's brows lifted as she glanced at Lacey. "You did say you could start right away?"

When Lacey nodded, her new boss led her through a doorway, saying over her shoulder, "Good. Saturday is our least busy day."

Now in the main part of the bakery, she indicated the college-age girl behind the counter. "Jen, this is Lacey Barnes. She'll be helping you during our morning rush for the next few weeks."

As Sue gave Lacey a brief rundown of her duties, thoughts of the starving dog stayed with her. She hated the idea of that poor creature fending for itself.

When her short interview ended, Lacey left the bakery and glanced around. Normally, back alleys were unkempt and dirty. Not this one. There were no weeds peeking through the mulched ground underneath the bushes, nor was there any litter strewn about that usually accompanied back-alley trash bins.

She drove out of the parking lot, keeping an eye out for any sign of the dog without success. But she did note that every storefront was freshly painted, and the windows clean of fingerprints and mud-splattered drops from yesterday's rain. A stray seemed so out of place in this affluent neighborhood. She doubted it had rabies.

The least Lacey could do was make sure it had food. She made a U-turn and headed in the direction of the pet superstore a few blocks away. After buying a bag of food and a plastic bowl, she made her way back to the Dumpster. She quickly set out a half-full bowl of food next to the spot she'd last spied the dog.

Her plan was to befriend the poor mutt over the next few days. Once that happened, she'd concentrate on finding it a good home.

Happy with her decision, her thoughts turned to Cade, and her tummy did flipflops as she drove to his house. She'd see him in less than an hour.

The next forty-five minutes dragged. When he finally did make it home, Lacey practically ran to meet him in the foyer.

"Did you sleep okay last night?" he asked giving her a warm smile.

Tongue-tied, she nodded, praying her grin didn't appear sappy. Cade wore jeans and a sports shirt that accentuated his lean, muscular build. He could easily pass for a model selling men's cologne, which matched Brandy and her size-two body selling women's cologne. Another reason he and the model were suited for each other.

Even as a teen, Lacey had never fit into a size two. Her hips were too wide and her breasts weren't big enough to give her an hourglass shape. Long ago, she'd come to terms with being a pear.

"How's the job search going?" Cade's voice brought her out of musings.

"Good," Lacey said cheerfully, explaining about her newfound job that helped with her ruse.

"By the way, I won't be here for dinner tonight." He gave her an apologetic shrug. "I have a date. With Brandy."

"Oh." Talk about a mood killer. If she said anything more, he'd be able to sense her disappointment. Lacey had no reason to be disappointed. Cade was just being nice, nothing more.

Thankfully, Camila's announcement that lunch was on the table interrupted the awkward moment that ensued.

"After you." Cade indicated for Lacey to go ahead of him.

The warmth in his gaze was back, and she couldn't help responding to it. Maybe he'd never see her as a girlfriend, but that didn't mean she couldn't enjoy his company. There was plenty of time to get over her infatuation with him.

Later. In the new year. When she was busy starting her new business.

In the meantime, she had to keep to her charade of moving to Atlanta.

<<>>

Later that night, Lacey sat at the dining room table in the same chair as only hours ago. Only this time, she was all alone.

Cade was out with Brandy, and Lacey missed him. More than she should.

She toyed with the spaghetti Camila had prepared earlier. Her appetite had all but disappeared. After twenty minutes of pretending to eat, she pushed away from the table and headed for her room, intending to read. She also planned to search the Internet for some apartment leads in case Cade asked about it. Wouldn't do to let him think she was abusing his hospitality.

A knock on her bedroom door sometime later pulled Lacey's attention out of the book she'd been reading on her e-reader.

"Lacey? Are you awake?"

A thrill shot through her as she jumped up to open the door. "Hi. I wasn't expecting you to be back so early."

He shrugged. "Brandy needs her beauty sleep."

"Oh." *Of course she does.*

"She's leaving at the crack of dawn for Miami, and has to be on the set at nine a.m. I don't have to be up so early, and I was hoping you might join me for a nightcap."

She shouldn't. Lacey knew darn well she shouldn't. Yet, his expression was so hopeful that she found herself agreeing.

Lacey had always loved him. Had never stopped these past ten years, and nothing on God's green earth was going to keep her from spending every available moment with him.

The time for regret would come later. When she was all alone again. At that point, she'd be too busy with starting her business to moon over him.

<<>>

Early the next morning, Lacey was up and dressed when a knock sounded. Thinking it was Camila, she rushed to open the door. "I don't have time for breakfast . . . Cade?" Her eyes grew big and she took a step back, surprised to see him standing there with a tray.

"Not even for a quick cup of coffee?"

A stronger person might be able to ignore that devil-may-care smile. But not her. Not when his eyes were alight with an invitation to dance a jig, and the urge to join in was all encompassing. Both always made her think she was special.

"When you put it that way, how can I refuse?" Lacey stood aside as he strode toward the table, and silently watched while he poured two cups before joining him and taking one.

Cade took a seat across from her and held up his cup. "To a successful first day."

"I'll drink to that."

They sipped and talked in front of the window, a view of the garden as a backdrop. Memories of other times they'd just sit and talk about everything and anything flooded back. It was as if the ten-year gap had never happened.

Eventually, Lacey confided in him about the dog she'd seen the day before that needed help. "I bought some food and plan on befriending him."

"I'll help you find a home for it."

Of course he'd offer. Cade had a soft spot for animals just like she did.

Lacey drained her cup and glanced at her watch. "Ooh, gotta go. Otherwise, I'll be late."

Laughing, Cade stood. "Can't have that." He followed her out of her room, down the stairs, and all the way out to her car.

He held her door open and watched as she buckled herself in. "We'll spend the afternoon together when you get off work. Do you still run?"

"Yeah, I do." In high school, she was on the cross-country team. Cade used to run with her all the time back then. He was faster, and helped her increase her speed enough to be a contender for her team.

His heart-stopping grin, the one that turned her insides to mush, was back. "Good. Let's see if you've still got it."

"I'd like that."

Smiling, she turned the key. If only she were immune to the man. Still, she couldn't deny how happy she felt at that moment.

Her smile stayed in place the entire drive to the bakery. Before going inside, she filled up the bowl, to the brim this time. There was still no sign of the dog, but Lacey felt confident that she could befriend him before her job at the bakery ended.

"Oh good, you're here. Grab an apron," Jen said as Lacey walked through the back-room door that led behind the counter. "Usually Saturdays aren't that busy, but not today."

Lacey did as instructed. Thoughts of the dog and Cade were replaced with learning her role. She found she enjoyed the mindless busy work.

Suddenly the store was empty of customers, when not even ten minutes earlier, the tables had been full and a few people had lingered at the counter. It was as if a bell had rung, telling everyone it was time to go.

Jen glanced at her watch. "Thanks, Lacey. Your shift is over. I'm glad Sue hired you. I'll see you on Monday?"

"Count on it," Lacey said before hurrying out to her car.

Her gaze flew to the Dumpster and the bowl. An empty bowl. She rushed to grab the bag of dog food and filled it up. Unwilling to let the dog go hungry again, she'd make a trip back in the morning.

Cade was already dressed in running gear when she let herself in his front door.

"I'll only be a minute." She turned to run up the stairs, taking them two at a time. After donning a T-shirt, leggings, and running shoes, she grabbed a sweatshirt, pleased that she'd had the good sense to pack them.

They headed out. Like earlier that morning, their conversation was easy and flowing. Cade talked about his latest project.

"You know it's Christmastime," she said. "When're you going to put up your tree?"

"I wasn't planning on it."

She stopped in mid-stride and sent him a glaring look. "Surely, you're joking?"

He laughed good-naturedly and shook his head. "No. I don't feel festive enough."

"Where's your Christmas spirit?"

"Somewhere between here and Charleston, I'd imagine," he said, then took off running again.

She followed, but made it a point to rib him about not having a tree every chance she got.

By the fourth mile, he put up a hand, obviously trying to keep from laughing. "Enough already. I'll think about it, okay?"

"You do that. In the meantime, just remember—I expect nothing less than a tree and some decorations around the house." After speaking her piece, she sprinted the last block, making him work to catch up with her.

"You're faster than I remember." His breathing was labored as he bent over and put his hands on his knees.

"No. I think you're just getting old."

"Ha." Straightening, he hip-bumped her and caught her gaze. "Bite your tongue, woman."

Suddenly, all teasing left his expression, and his eyes focused on her mouth for what seemed like forever.

Heat streaked up her neck and warmed her cheeks. All too quickly, the intensity of his look was gone. Lacey wasn't sure if it had been real or her imagination running on overtime.

She cleared her throat. "I enjoyed that. We need to do it again sometime." She couldn't resist adding, "If only to get you back into shape."

He opened his front door, tsk-tsking. "First you find fault with my lack of Christmas spirit, and then you insult me by reminding me how out of shape I am."

Laughing, she followed him inside. "It's a good thing I'm here then, isn't it?"

"My thoughts exactly." The humor in his voice warmed her as she headed for her room to take a shower.

Chapter 7

Lacey awoke the next morning to a darkened room. Her gaze wandered to the windows, where only gloom and dreariness peered in from outside. Raindrops ran down the glass, replacing the sun's rays of the day before. A chill now permeated the air.

As much as she'd love to dive back under the covers to spend more time in bed, thoughts of the stray dog wouldn't let her. If she was cold in a warm house, he or she had to be cold and miserable in the storm raging outside. Hurriedly, she brushed her teeth, showered, and was headed downstairs within ten minutes.

Cade was already seated at the dining room table when she strode in.

"Good morning." His usual smile, one that could chase away any winter gloominess, accompanied his greeting.

Camila came out of the kitchen, carrying a pot of coffee. "Sit. I bring you some breakfast."

Lacey was dying to bask in the warmth of Cade's smile and enjoy one of Camila's breakfasts, but she shook her head. "I don't have time. I need to find the stray dog."

"A dog?" Camila's voice registered surprise. "I love dogs. I lost my Angelina a month ago."

"How about adopting this one?" Cade said, adding, "I'll throw in a vet visit, complete with shots and spaying or neutering."

"I'll think about it," she said on her way to the kitchen.

Cade jumped up and followed Lacey. "I promised to help, remember?" At the hallway closet, he stopped long enough to pull out two rain jackets. "We'll take my car."

"Your Jaguar?" Lacey spun around, struggling to keep the surprise off her face. "The dog's going to be wet and muddy."

"It's a car, Lacey."

"A nice expensive car with leather seats."

"Which means rain and mud should clean up easily."

"What if this dog scratches it?"

"I'll get it fixed." His nonchalant shrug added to the statement.

Of course Cade would say something like that. He'd always cared about a person's feelings or making sure animals were treated well, Lacey thought as Camila came rushing toward them, carrying towels and a blanket.

"The bambino will be cold and wet."

As she handed them to Cade, Lacey could tell that the housekeeper already considered the dog hers. Even funnier, Lacey had a sneaking suspicion that the housekeeper might have to fight Cade for ownership.

No wonder she'd fallen in love with him all those years ago.

Wipers swished back and forth, slinging torrents of rainwater off the glass as Cade drove in the direction of the bakery.

"Do you think we'll be able to find the dog in this mess?" Lacey's tone lacked enthusiasm. The idea was amplified when Cade noted the worry etched into her beautiful features.

"He or she has probably holed up someplace dry." That's what he'd do if he were a dog. One could only hope this dog had such a place, he thought, staring at the swinging stoplight distorted through the wet glass.

Eventually, he spotted the bakery. He slowed to a crawl and began circling the block. "Keep your eyes peeled on the alleyways, and look for anywhere a dog could hide."

As they neared the bakery again, Lacey pointed. "Check the alley behind the bakery. I'll put out some more food. Maybe that will help draw him out."

Cade did as Lacey suggested, turning onto the road that led to the parking lot in the rear. When he came to a stop next to the Dumpster, Lacey jumped out. The worst of this wave of rain had passed, leaving behind a steady drizzle.

As Lacey filled the empty bowl with more food, Cade climbed out and joined her. Slowly, he pivoted, his gaze searching as he moved.

Less than a minute later, movement from behind the Dumpster caught his attention. Then he heard a whimper.

"Here, boy—or girl," he called.

The whimper turned into a louder yelp as the dog appeared, drenched and mud-caked. The stray hesitated as Cade continued talking to him in a soothing tone. Apparently deciding Cade was the lesser of the two evils, the dog cautiously began belly-crawling toward them.

Cade hurried back to the car to grab the towels. He handed one to Lacey, and the two of them started to dry off the bedraggled animal.

Once they got as much water and mud off the animal as possible, Lacey, who'd retrieved the blanket, wrapped him, or rather her. It was obviously female, and not a very old one at that.

"There you go, sweetie," Lacey cooed. "You just curl up. We'll have you warm in no time."

Cade grunted and opened the car door. "You know she doesn't understand what you're saying."

"Doesn't matter. It's my tone of voice that tells her I mean her no harm."

The dog crawled to the center of the backseat and circled a couple of times before making herself comfortable. In the next instant, she was sound asleep.

Lacey's smug expression shouted *I told you so*.

Cade only laughed and shut the rear door before opening the passenger's. "Let's get her home." He raced around to the other side. Once seated, he started the car, then turned to Lacey. "Then we can make arrangements for having her checked out with a vet."

"Thanks, Cade. I really appreciate your help. It means a lot." Lacey then leaned in and gave him a kiss on the cheek.

Her essence invaded his space and surrounded him with warmth. Her spicy scent hit his nose and traveled from there to his groin.

She smelled like cinnamon and vanilla. He remembered the scent from when she was in high school. Funny that she would still wear it, he mused, as memories of a more carefree time flashed through his mind, like one of those electronic gizmos that kept repeating a sequence.

As he drove out of the parking lot, Lacey asked, "Have you thought any more about going home for Christmas?" When he didn't answer right away, she added, "Remember that last Christmas in your junior year? I thought you'd never forgive me for teasing you about your haircut."

"I got over it." He hated the cut more than she did. It was the catalyst for making the decision to leave the Citadel. "And yes, I've thought about going home for Christmas." He smiled, then broke out in another quick laugh.

"My joke wasn't that funny."

"To me it was," he said evasively, unwilling to answer honestly. Lacey was like a dog with a bone, only her jaw was stronger than that of most dogs. Telling her that would only hurt her feelings. "I'm waffling, as usual, and haven't made up my mind."

Some things never changed, and one of those things was that they still knew each other's little quirks. They'd spent years developing that kind of friendship. It was nice to be reminded that there were plenty of good times worth remembering. Funny how most of those times also included Lacey.

Slowing for a red light, he gave her a considering look. He couldn't deny that he'd felt more at home in his house since she'd accepted his offer of a room.

Brandy was always complaining about how crappy everything looked during remodeling. Due to her busy schedule, she never saw a completed house. True, there had only been one other completion, and he had tried to encourage her to see his accomplishment, but she was more interested in his fashion retail company. When she had finally spared the time, it was too late. The house had closed within days of selling. Some wealthy people didn't do mortgages, paying cash instead, and closings happened much quicker than the few weeks to a month or longer when a loan was involved.

Settling down and staying put in one of his houses sounded appealing all of a sudden. His current house was starting to grow on him. Unfortunately, the thought of sharing it with Brandy didn't sit as well in his psyche as it should have. He certainly hadn't minded sharing it with Lacey. It was definitely a tough thought to chew on. Later.

Cade pulled into his long driveway. After shutting off the ignition, he turned to Lacey. "Since the weather is too wet to run, how about going ice skating after we get the dog settled?"

Lacey's expression went from a smile to a frown in a nanosecond. "I've never been."

"Then it's settled. It's never too late to learn."

"I have serious doubts about that last statement. I wasn't a very good roller skater either."

The thought of helping her learn, while she leaned on him for support, should have been a warning that his feelings for Lacey might be getting out of hand—very similar to feelings years ago that caused him to bail on her.

Discarding the notion as ridiculous, he raced around to help her out of the car before seeing to the dog. He hadn't bailed on her. He'd escaped a tyrant of a father, who was pounding his round son into a square peg of a job.

Besides, he needn't worry. He had plenty of time to figure out his future with Brandy. He was just enjoying Lacey's company.

<<>>

During the next week, while Brandy was in Miami, Lacey spent as much time with Cade as his schedule allowed. Lacey no longer worried about the dog. After the vet had issued an all clear, Camila had adopted their stray, naming her Lucky.

Thank God Lacey had the job at the bakery, otherwise waiting for him would have been torture. They went jogging if the weather permitted, and ice skating when it rained. Who knew ice skating could be so exhilarating...and romantic. Memories of their outing and Cade holding onto her for most of the hour resurfaced. She hadn't laughed so hard in ages. Cade was so much fun, and Lacey fell further and further in love with him.

When Lacey continued to question Cade about why he didn't have a Christmas tree, he'd give his stock answer about not feeling festive enough. But, he'd eventually caved, telling her that since she'd arrived, his Christmas spirit had returned. He also insisted that trudging through a snow-covered tree farm was the only way to go, if only for the experience. And why would Lacey disagree when it meant going on another adventure?

The day was cool but clear as they drove to North Carolina and the Smoky Mountains. A little over two hours out of Atlanta, they stopped for lunch at a funky restaurant in Franklin. According to Cade, they still had a couple of hours to their destination.

As Lacey ordered, she tried to think of a way to broach the subject of returning to Johns Island for the holidays more forcefully than she already had. He'd hemmed and hawed at her previous attempts. With only ten days left until Christmas, time was running out.

Once the waiter took their orders and was out of earshot, she said, "Have you thought any more about my suggestion?"

"What suggestion?"

"I'm going back to South Carolina for Christmas in a few days, and I'd love it if you could come too. We could drive together."

"I'm still considering it. It's time I let go of the past." He reached for her hand that was lying on top of the table and gave it a little squeeze. Then he patted it. "And I have you to thank. It'll be nice to see everyone."

Lacey subdued the desire to do a little dance. Instead, she grinned. "You won't be sorry."

"I'm not sure about timing, so you should go ahead and make your own plans. If I can swing getting away so soon, I'll be happy to drive with you."

For the rest of the meal, Lacey was in the best mood. Nothing could dampen her spirits. In fact, the day got better as they continued their grand adventure deep into the Smokies.

The higher they went, the more snow they encountered. Still, the roads were clear.

Eventually, Cade turned onto a winding, narrow road. A few miles later, they came to the entrance of the Smoky Mountain Christmas Tree Farm.

"How did you ever learn about this place?" Her voice held much of the awe she was feeling as she looked around.

"I googled it."

They climbed out of the car. The song "It's Beginning to Look a Lot Like Christmas" played over the loudspeaker. As far as the eye could see was row after row of trees, just waiting for the right owner to chop one down and take it home.

Cade waved for her to go ahead. "We have lots to choose from, so let's get going before it gets too late. We still have a four-hour drive ahead of us." He pointed to one. "That looks like a perfect tree."

Just like a man to zero in on the first one he saw that looked okay. Lacey shook her head and kept walking. "No. We aren't going to settle on something as important as a Christmas tree."

As she stepped into the fifth row, a snowball hit her clean on the back of her neck. Laughing and not to be outdone, she grabbed a fistful of snow and made a ball. Using one of the trees as cover, she lobbed one directly at Cade's face. Bull's-eye.

"Oh, you wanna play dirty?"

Squealing with more laughter, she started running, but the six inches of snow on the ground hampered her efforts. Cade reached her in three steps before he tackled her to the ground, managing to buffer the impact with his body at the same time.

Lacey's laughter died when she pushed up and noted what was in his gaze.

Desire. Pure and simple. Mirroring exactly what was in her heart.

Just as quickly as it had sprung up, it was gone. As she continued staring down at him, she wasn't sure if it had been wishful thinking on her part, or if he'd felt the same thing she had.

"We should get our tree and go," Cade said, setting her aside and standing. He bent to help her up. As he brushed snow off his jeans, another couple came into view, so it was just as well nothing had happened.

Still, as Lacey followed him back to their tree, she couldn't shake the disappointment that lurked right behind her common sense. She knew darn well she'd have kissed him if he'd just raised his head one more inch.

The only thing the last few minutes had taught her was that when it came to Cade Duval, she was a fool in love.

Chapter 8

The first hour of the trip back to Atlanta was made in silence, during which time Cade regretted his stupidity. He'd come too close to kissing her. Bad enough that he'd almost ruined a perfectly good friendship over lust, but what really disgusted him was the desire to do so hadn't abated. In fact, it grew stronger when she started talking and joking again after her initial silence.

It was definitely tough thought to chew on, he decided as he drove up his long, winding driveway. As he hit the garage-door opener, he noted a taxi off to the side.

"What the hell?"

When he stopped the car inside the garage, he saw Brandy climb out of the yellow car and start marching up to his Jag.

Deciding to meet her halfway, Cade switched off the ignition and hurried out of the car. Nearing her, he said, "Brandy. I didn't expect you until next week."

She glared at him accusingly. "I texted you. And left messages."

Damn. Cade pulled the dead cell phone out of his pocket. "Sorry. I was on all morning, and I forgot to take my charger with me to North Carolina." Actually, he hadn't even given it a second thought thanks to Lacey's company.

Her nod indicated the roof of the Jag. "I see you have a tree. I thought you didn't like them."

"I changed my mind. I've also changed my mind about going home for Christmas." Might as well get it all out now so she could be angry about that as well.

Her eyes lit up. "We're going to Charleston for Christmas?" She practically leaped into his arms and locked lips with his. Then she broke the kiss and said with much enthusiasm, "Oh Cade, that's fabulous. I've been looking forward to meeting your family."

49

Not having the heart, or the guts, to tell her he would rather go without her, he glanced over her shoulder at Lacey, who'd exited the car, and offered her a wan smile.

Somehow, this entire thing had blown up in his face. He didn't want Brandy to meet his family, especially now that he had doubts about their relationship. After spending these last carefree days with Lacey, he'd come to one conclusion. A few things had to change between Brandy and him if they were to continue long-term.

Then again, this trip would give him the perfect opportunity to explain his position.

Lacey hurried into the house from the garage door, drawing Brandy's gaze.

"What's she doing here?" Brandy's tone was harsh. Her angry eyes shot daggers at him.

Despite the fact that Brandy's mien wasn't becoming, Cade swallowed a lump of guilt that had lodged in his throat. At this point, he was damn sure Brandy had reason to worry.

"I told you she's an old family friend. No friend of mine stays in a hotel, which means she's been staying here."

The day had been wonderful and more than relaxing. Cade hadn't realized how much fun the adventure of finding the perfect tree could be.

If he was being truthful, and why lie to himself, he couldn't deny that on the entire drive home, he'd looked forward to decorating said tree with Lacey—not with Brandy. He'd also planned a romantic dinner with her, along with plying her with much eggnog and bourbon. Whether things heated up from there would have been totally up to her. But since he was being honest, he'd been hoping she'd be willing.

What kind of friend did that make him? Not a very good one, that was for sure. Or boyfriend.

He spent a few minutes calming Brandy down, fully aware his evening would be a total bust.

"Let's go inside. I'll hurry and change while you decide where to go for dinner. Okay?"

The peace offering seemed to work, and Brandy nodded. She quickly dismissed the cab, but halfway up the walkway, she started whining again.

"Why can't she stay in a hotel?"

Cade sighed, knowing full well the *she* was Lacey. "She's my guest for as long as she wants to be here." Besides, he didn't really want her to stay in a hotel.

When he went to tell Camila, he was going out to dinner, she informed him that Lacey was having hers in her room.

Damn. He quickly changed into something dressier that matched Brandy's dress. On his way down the curved stairway, he saw Brandy pacing like a caged tiger. When she glanced up and their gazes met, he suddenly felt like her prey.

What a silly thought.

He probably should put the brakes on taking her home to South Carolina, but with her there, he could keep Lacey at arm's length. It was getting harder and harder to restrain the desire to take her in his arms and make love to her. He wasn't about to destroy their friendship over sex like some stupid kid who couldn't keep it in his pants.

Thankfully, his evening with Brandy ended early. She never stayed over at his house, claiming it was too much trouble to lug her suitcase of essentials for her beauty routine back and forth. Apparently, she was waiting until he gave her closet space and a key before she'd consider it. It had always seemed premature in their relationship, and now he was pretty sure it wasn't going in that direction.

Needing space to think, he made an excuse of having to work to avoid spending the night with Brandy.

Now home, he climbed up the stairs, wondering if Lacey was still awake. On the second-floor landing, he looked down the hallway. A twinge of disappointment struck when there was no light under her door.

He sighed and turned to go into his room, slowly undoing his tie as he went and feeling lonelier than he ever had.

A few days later, Lacey left at the break of dawn for Johns Island, having said her goodbyes at the bakery the day before and letting them know she was leaving Atlanta and retuning home for Christmas.

Since Brandy's return, Cade hadn't been around much. The two were driving to Charleston later that morning. Not wanting to bump into him, she'd packed her bags and had tiptoed out of his house like a thief in the night, intending never to return.

The entire trip she kept wiping tears from her eyes, admonishing herself for falling under his spell. Again. She had only herself to blame. He'd never led her on. He'd been up front and honest about his relationship with Brandy.

Brandy. Even the name conjured up a bimbo who didn't deserve a guy like Cade. Still, he was old enough to make up his own mind.

The Kia Rio left a trail of dust in its wake once she turned onto the dirt road that led to Duval Plantation. When she neared the big house, she slowed and parked in her usual spot on the far right side of the garage.

It was past noon, and having not stopped at all on the drive, Lacey was surprised to realize she was hungry. As she entered the separate door in the garage that led to the apartment she shared with her grandfather, she spotted Ms. Maddie, who must have heard her car's approach.

Bucking up and pasting a smile on her face, she stopped. "I'm back. Guess you figured that out."

"Where's Cade?"

"Don't worry. I was successful in my mission. Cade's on his way."

"Mission, what mission? Mother? What does she mean, Cade's on his way?"

Both women turned at the voice. Cade's dad stood a few feet away.

"Martin? I didn't realize you were here."

"Obviously. What's this about Cade?"

In her firmest Ms. Maddie tone, the one that brooked no argument, she said, "It's rude to eavesdrop."

He snorted. "I wasn't eavesdropping. I was looking for you and just happened to overhear your conversation."

"I wanted to surprise you."

"My son's coming here?" His tone went from annoyance to pure pleasure.

"Yes. For Christmas. Isn't that right, Lacey?"

Lacey nodded. "He should be here in a few hours. With a woman he's been seeing."

"What?" Ms. Maddie's gaze flashed shock until she banked the expression and smiled. "I didn't realize he was seeing anyone."

"Wait a minute. Let me get this straight. Tell me you didn't send Lacey to Atlanta on some harebrained scheme to play matchmaker?"

Ms. Maddie threw her shoulders back. "I don't know what you're talking about," she sputtered, her cheeks turning a darker shade of pink.

"You should know better than to interfere in his life after the way he stormed out of here ten years ago."

"No." Ms. Maddie shook her head. "You and I both know he left because of you."

"Just dig the knife in a little deeper, why don't you," Martin said before striding with purpose back into the house.

Having witnessed their little spat, Lacey wanted to disappear into the woodwork. "I think I'll go unpack." She turned to go, but stopped in her tracks and spun back around at Ms. Maddie's voice.

"Wait."

Ms. Maddie walked up to her, laid a hand on her shoulder, and squeezed. "I'm really sorry. I'd hoped things would turn out differently."

"Excuse me?" Lacey's jaw dropped open. She couldn't believe her ears. Had Martin been right about Ms. Maddie's intention?

"Oh, come now," Ms. Maddie said, waving her hand as if brushing aside Lacey's confusion. "You didn't think I'd send you to Atlanta without knowing about that torch you've held for Cade all these years?" She made eye contact and added, "Plus, he hadn't become involved with anyone, well…until now. I just figured he hadn't realized his attachment to you. I thought maybe your showing up would give him a little push in your direction."

"I'm sure you meant well, but considering how things have turned out, I'd appreciate it if from now on you'd mind your own business." After getting the words out, Lacey resumed her exit, only this time she practically ran toward the apartment door.

"Lacey."

Hand on the doorknob, she looked back. "What?"

"I deposited the amount we discussed into your account the day after you left Johns Island. You can start your business anytime, and I'll be happy to assist you any way I can."

Tears filled Lacey's eyes. "Thanks."

What good would having a business do her when her heart was breaking?

Once upstairs in the apartment she shared with her grandfather, she made a beeline for her bedroom, praying she wouldn't see him until she pulled herself together.

Thankfully, he was out mending a fence they'd put up a few months ago.

Commotion in the yard a while later drew Lacey out of her melancholy thoughts, and she moved to the window. Cade had arrived. He parked his Jag right under Lacey's bedroom window so she had a bird's-eye view of him helping Brandy out of the car.

His aunts, uncles, and cousins had heard of his impending arrival, and were all present and accounted for to greet the returning prodigal son. Cade's dad and grandmother stood at the head of the group.

Lacey never felt lonely until that moment when she realized she'd always be an interloper.

<<>>

Cade was miserable. Had been the entire five-hour drive to Johns Island. In the confines of the car with Brandy, he'd realized one thing. He didn't want to be with Brandy any longer, and he needed to tell her the truth. And soon, judging by the predatory way the woman made herself at home.

He looked around for Lacey. Finally, he found the nerve to ask his grandmother, "Have you seen Lacey?"

Madelyn gave him a considering look. "She arrived a couple of hours ago. Don't trifle with her, or you'll have me to deal with." She then turned and walked inside, leaving him staring after her openmouthed.

It was time to tell Brandy the truth. Then beg for Lacey's forgiveness.

Cade found Brandy in the great room, surrounded by all of his male cousins. From his vantage point, she looked to be in her element. She laughed at something his cousin Shane said, and then did the hair-flip thing that told a guy she was interested in him. So maybe Brandy wasn't into Cade any more than he was into her. And wouldn't that make his job of dropping her easier.

"Brandy, can I talk you?"

"Sure."

When she made no effort to move, he added, "Outside. In private."

Wearing a sullen look, she nodded and followed him out the main door of his grandmother's huge house and onto the front landing. Hopefully, the others would stay inside.

"I realize that you may have gotten the wrong impression about this trip. I came here to be with my family for Christmas, but I wasn't planning on introducing you to them this soon in our relationship."

"What?" Her gaze narrowed as she studied his face with the precision of an IRS agent looking for deception in a return. "Then why did you bring me?"

He shrugged. "It just sorta happened," he said for want of anything better. He cleared his throat and went for broke. "Actually, since you've been gone on this last shoot, I've begun to have reservations concerning us." He motioned between the two of them with his hand.

"Wait a minute." She shook her head and her confusion cleared. "Are you breaking up with me?"

"Yes. No." He slammed a hand through his hair. "I don't know."

"But things were great between us." Her gaze narrowed into slits, and a vicious look came into her eyes. "It's because of that witch who came to visit you, isn't it?"

"No, it's not," he said in a resigned voice, wishing he didn't have to do this now.

"I don't believe you. You were happy before *she* came along."

"Yeah, I can't deny that. But she only reminded me of how I used to be and how much I've changed. I don't like who I've become, so I'm making changes. One of those changes is you. I don't love you, and I doubt you love me. I also don't like being micromanaged."

"I don't micromanage you."

"You could have fooled me. Hell, I even got roped into bringing you here for Christmas when it was the furthest thing from my mind."

Just then, raised voices came from the direction of the open garage a few feet away.

Cade turned toward the door in order to hear them better. It sounded a lot like his grandmother and Joe, her caretaker, having a heated argument. He held up a hand to stop Brandy from what she was about to say after overhearing his name and Lacey's as the voices grew louder.

"I didn't know this would happen when I sent her to Atlanta to bring Cade back, Joe."

"Why didn't you just leave well enough alone?"

"I thought I was doing the right thing. Besides, she was paid handsomely. At least now she can move on with her life and start that event-planning company she's always dreamed of having."

Wait a minute. Cade was brought up short and could barely believe what the two were saying. Lacey was paid to go to Atlanta? To bring him back into the fold?

The realization cut like a knife straight into his heart and made him feel like a total fool. The two lowered their voices, and he couldn't make out more. Soon, they must have left the garage entirely because it was totally quiet.

"Well now. Just look at who isn't so lily-white in all of this. And you're actually dumping me for her?" Brandy's smug expression made her look almost ugly as she added, "I'm out of here. I'll call Uber for a ride to the airport. Who knows? I might even be able to hook up with the photographer who wanted to know if he could call me. Don't expect me to jump for joy when you come to your senses and come crawling back to me, either." With that said, she spun on her heel and headed for the house, her head held high.

Cade rubbed his temples, suddenly feeling a headache coming on. He'd have to be desperate to crawl back to her. Unfortunately, it was something he recognized too late.

He looked up at the window that he knew was Lacey's bedroom. Maybe he'd heard it all wrong. Before he made any rash judgments, he had to find out by going to the horse's mouth and hearing what this particular horse, or female, had to say for herself.

He picked up a few smaller pebbles and lobbed them at the window. After several attempts, Lacey finally looked out. He motioned for her to come down.

Cade didn't have to wait long before she stood in front of him.

"Did you want to see me? Is that why you were throwing rocks at my window?"

"They were only pebbles, and I didn't throw them that hard." He tried to smile, but his lips wouldn't curl in the right direction, so he gave up all pretense of joviality. "I need to know something, and I want you to be honest."

Lacey looked him straight in the eye and nodded. "Okay." Her eyes were a little red and her face was puffy, like she'd been crying.

Cade swallowed a huge lump of compassion, annoyed for feeling anything empathetic toward her. Before wasting any more emotion on her, he'd wait for her answer.

"Did my grandmother pay you to bring me back home?"

Her cheeks reddened and she couldn't keep meeting his gaze, which didn't bode well for his heart.

"Before I say yes or no, you need to know there were extenuating circumstances," she whispered.

"I don't give a flying fig about extenuating circumstances. Just answer the damn question. Did you receive money for ensuring I'd be here for Christmas?"

Still staring at the ground, she nodded slowly. "But I can explain."

He didn't wait for more, just turned and walked away. With every step, his heart crushed further to the point of numbness. It was difficult to breathe.

How he made it into the house and through the sea of Duval cousins, aunts, and uncles without hitting one of them, he didn't know. All he knew was that he had to be alone. And fast. The dock on the marsh was the best place for his purposes.

"Hey, Cade." Shane, the Duval cousin closest to his own age, yelled at him.

Sucking in needed air, Cade stopped and turned.

"Did you just drop that model who rode with you all the way from Atlanta?"

Cade nodded. "Yes. But I'd rather not talk about it. If you don't mind, I'd prefer to be alone."

"Sure, no problem." Before Shane left, he asked, "So it's okay if I look her up?"

Cade gave a backward wave. "Have at it."

In his opinion, Brandy and Shane made the perfect shallow couple. And they'd probably have perfectly shallow kids together.

Chapter 9

As Lacey watched Cade walk away, she didn't think her heart could bear it. She headed to the one place she could be alone. Upstairs to hide in her room. The faster she ran, the faster the tears fell.

Once inside, having her grandfather see her was her biggest concern. Unfortunately, he was coming out of the bathroom before she could make it to her bedroom.

"Lacey? What happened?"

"Nothing. Just leave me alone."

Madelyn was in the kitchen, giving the cook instructions on what to prepare for dinner that night. It looked like they were going to have a full table. She smiled and rubbed her hands together, intending to ask both Joe and Lacey to join them.

The scuttlebutt among the grandkids was that the woman Cade brought home had left in a huff. There was only one thing in Madelyn's mind that could cause such an event. Cade had feelings for Lacey, just as she'd suspected all these years. And Lacey obviously had feelings for him.

"Madelyn? I need to speak with you."

Recognizing the voice, she looked toward the doorway. She spent a moment surreptitiously studying Joe's strong facial features from the side as he stood with the erect bearing of the Air Force pilot he'd been long ago. A longing filled her as she remembered a time when they'd been lovers. Years before she married Martin's father. Joe had gone to Viet Nam, against her wishes. He'd gotten a college deferment, but after two years, he felt he had to do his part for the country when so many were against it. His decision had sealed both their fates. Shaking the sad thoughts, she said, "Joe? I was just on my way to ask you and Lacey to join us for dinner."

"Lacey isn't feeling well." He came up to her and grabbed her by the elbow. "I really need to talk to you."

"If this is about Cade and Lacey, you don't have to worry about Cade. He sent that bimbo packing."

She tried to yank out of his grasp, but he held firm until they were outside in the pool area. Dusk was near, and the cooler temperatures kept everyone inside. Plus, there was some football game on that held the grandkids' attention.

Out of range of prying ears, she stopped and looked at Joe. "What's wrong?"

"Lacey is beside herself with grief, and your grandson is the reason."

"No. That can't be." This wasn't how she'd envisioned the night would end when she saw the last of Cade's girlfriend. "Let me go and find out what's what with Cade. I saw him go down to his favorite spot about ten minutes ago."

"Fine. But if you don't fix this, I'm resigning."

"You can't do that."

"Try me," he said in a voice that was dead serious before he spun around and headed toward the garage.

"Stubborn man," she whispered going to do his bidding. If he left, she'd be devastated.

Madelyn saw Cade's dark, brooding form in silhouette at the end of the dock as she neared the first step.

"Did you come to gloat?" he asked as she got closer.

"No. I came to explain and to ask your forgiveness."

She sat down next to him and let her legs swing back and forth, as he was doing. It reminded her of all those days when he was a little tyke and they'd sit like this. She doubted he remembered, and even if he did, it wouldn't do much good since he seemed hurt.

"I'm sorry, Cade. I shouldn't have interfered in your life."

"I've never heard you apologize before now."

"Yes, well, don't let on. Otherwise, my reputation will be destroyed." After a moment of silence, she said, "Why are you here? And why is Lacey up there crying her eyes out?"

"I can't believe you paid her to come to Atlanta and ruin my life."

"Would it help if you knew that I coerced her? I offered her money at first, and she turned me down. Cold. Then I threw in that I was firing her grandfather."

Cade snorted. "Even I know that's an empty threat."

"Yes, but she didn't. Besides, Cade, I knew her secret."

That caught his attention and he glanced at her. "Well? What is it?"

"She's always loved you. And I had a sneaking suspicion that you felt something for her. Maybe not love, but you always treated her with the utmost kindness, and—" She broke off and shrugged. "It seemed more than brotherly to me."

He heaved a loud sigh. "Since we're being honest here, I should tell you that Lacey made me realize how stupid I am to hold the grudge against Dad."

"That's a miracle in and of itself. I think your dad is ready to admit he was wrong." She squeezed his hand. "You need to talk to him. And you need to talk to Lacey. Christmas is the time for forgiveness and a time to love. Don't close your heart any more than you already have."

After giving her advice, she tried to stand. She laughed when she practically fell in the marsh. If not for Cade, who'd jumped up to add his support, she would have.

"Guess I'm not as agile as I once was."

"You're still young at heart. And that's what matters." He bent to give her a kiss on the cheek. "Thanks, Grandmother. I love you, and I'm glad you went to such great lengths to bring me to my senses."

"Don't wait too long to make amends. I'm not going to live forever."

<<>>

Cade sat back down and contemplated what his grandmother had just told him. She was right, except he wasn't quite sure of how to go about making amends. With his father or with Lacey. After much thought, he decided on the direct approach.

He quickly found his dad in the great room. Martin was playing pool with Shane.

"Dad, can I talk to you?" he asked, leaning in so only his father could hear. The rest of the clan didn't need to know any more of his business than they already did.

Martin nodded. "Just let me finish this shot." After sinking two balls, then the eight ball, he set his pool cue on the shelf and held out his hand. "I believe you owe me a ten-spot."

"I've been hustled by my own uncle," Shane said good-naturedly as he pulled out a bill from his wallet and gave it to Martin.

Cade's dad stuck the bill in his wallet, then gave Cade his full attention. "Now, we can talk."

Cade led him into his grandmother's study.

"I want to be friends, Dad," he said. "I'd also like to apologize for staying away so long, and staying angry with you long after I'd proven you wrong."

Martin laughed. "And that you did, my son." Jingling keys in his pants pocket, he sighed before capturing Cade's gaze, one much like his own. "I'm the one who should apologize. I was just doing what I thought best after your mom died. I forgot how much she used to set me straight where you were concerned. I'm sorry I tried to make you into someone you weren't. It was easy for me to follow into my father's footsteps because he and I thought alike. You have your mother's artistic nature, and rather than try and quash it, I should have embraced it, if only to feel closer to her. I'm sorry."

His explanation and those two words had an amazing effect. *I'm sorry* went a long way toward healing wounds that had festered for a decade.

"I wish I hadn't waited so long to come home, Dad."

Martin pulled him into a bear hug, and Cade hugged him back. Hard. Love warmed him.

His dad stepped back and released him, then clapped him on the shoulder. "Now, go and find Lacey. I'd love it if you made her part of the family."

Jeez. Did everyone know about his feelings for her but him?

Still, Cade took the stairs two at a time to the apartment over the garage, intending to crawl if he had to for her forgiveness.

He pounded on the door. "Lacey, I'm sorry. I love you. I need you. Please forgive me," he yelled at the top of his lungs.

A long moment later, the door opened an inch. He almost lost it when he noted her tearstained face, knowing he was the cause.

"I'm so sorry I said the things I said. I was angry." The lump in his throat grew to the point of making it hard to swallow. He quickly blinked away moisture forming as his gaze sought hers. "Can you ever forgive me?"

The door opened another inch. The intensity with which she studied his face made him think she was weighing his sincerity. He realized right then his life meant nothing if she wasn't in it and he decided to go for broke. "I love you, Lacey. And I can't live without you. Will you marry me?"

The door flew open and Lacey flung herself into his arms, kissing him with wild abandon. "Yes, yes, yes. A thousand times yes."

Tightening his grip and twirling her around, he laughed. "What do you think of a Christmas wedding?"

Arms still latched around his neck, Lacey leaned back. "Can we do it that quickly?"

"We're Duvals. Of course we can. We'll have it here. With just close friends and family. I'm sure my grandmother will be up to the challenge."

It was still days before Christmas, but Cade glanced at the heavens, knowing without a doubt he'd experienced a Christmas miracle of the best kind.

A Christmas miracle in the Lowcountry.

Epilogue

Sunshine warmed her face, even as the crisp December breeze blew off the marsh. It was in the low seventies, the perfect temperature for a wedding.

Grinning with an urge to bay at the quarter moon on the horizon, Madelyn Duval stood in the back of the outdoor pavilion and surveyed her surroundings. Pots of camellias lined the garden, and vases of the same flowers graced the elegantly covered tables. Chairs were draped in matching off-white satin, and trimmed in red and green ribbon. The romantic ambience took every bit of Madelyn's time to create since being informed of Cade and Lacey's intention to marry on Christmas Day.

Of course, it helped to have the right connections—and money—although money never could buy happiness. Especially not the kind of happiness that only family provided. Having them all attend church together on one of the holiest days of the year gave Madelyn enough joy that she was certain it would last all year.

Finally, the music shifted, indicating her cue. She placed her hand through her grandson's bent arm and allowed Shane to escort her up the aisle to where Martin and the rest of her clan waited. Once she was seated, the organist paused as Shane took his seat before beginning the wedding march.

The small group stood and turned to watch the bride dressed in a sophisticated off-the-shoulder ivory satin-and-lace gown.

Lacey was all smiles as her grandfather walked her toward Cade and her future. Like all brides, she was a vision to behold, but Lacey was special.

Madelyn was proud of her part in bringing about this wedding. Joe's granddaughter and Cade would make beautiful children together. And she'd finally be a great-grandmother.

Humph, she thought, sparing Shane a sideways glance. Kids today were in no big hurry to find love. They didn't understand the importance of family. Shane wasn't much younger than his cousin Cade, but he dated and discarded many women—much like some of her friends bought and tossed out shoes after only wearing them a half dozen times.

Well, that was about to change. She'd make sure of it, or her name wasn't Madelyn Duval.

As her resolve strengthened and her back straightened, her gaze sought out Joe. He stood as regal as ever, reminding her once again of the past they'd once shared. If only he weren't so stubborn. She sighed and decided to be thankful for the miracles she'd already experienced.

Martin and Cade, her favorite grandson, had made their peace. Cade was marrying Lacey. And finally, her land would be safe in Cade's hands, once her time on this earth had ended.

Madelyn held her face up to the warmth of the sun and smiled. Yep. Lowcountry Christmas miracles were the best.

<<>The End<>>

Thank you for reading *A Lowcountry Christmas Miracle*. I hope you enjoyed it! If you did, please consider reviewing the story. Reviews help other readers find books. I appreciate all reviews, whether positive or negative. Share a link, tweet about it, Facebook it . . . everything helps in this new Internet world.

Check out the first book in A CHRISTMAS MIRACLE SERIES, A CHRISTMAS MIRACLE – Book 1, another heartwarming and uplifting short Christmas story to warm the heart during this cold holiday season...

Megan Jenkins isn't looking forward to Christmas. The holidays will forevermore remind her of what she had and lost. Her husband, and love of her life, died a few days after Christmas the year before, leaving her a young widow with a fatherless son to raise. During the course of this Christmas Eve, Megan experiences her own Christmas Miracle as she learns the true meaning of giving with the help of Kevin Murdock, a long-time friend who's always been there for her. A Christmas Miracle is based on a true story--a Christmas Eve adventure that had to be immortalized in this short story so it would never be forgotten. The circumstances and names have been changed. Any similarity to real persons, living or dead, is purely coincidental and not intended by the author.

If you would like to know when my next book is available, visit my website at www.sandyloyd.com and sign up for my newsletter. Or you can e-mail me at sandyloyd@twc.com, and I'll add you to my list so that you'll receive updates on new releases.

Like my Facebook page at www.facebook.com/sloydwrites, or follow me on Twitter at www.twitter.com/sloydwrites.

For an overview of the types of books she writes, turn the page.

About The Author

Sandy Loyd has worked and lived in some fabulous places in the US, including Northern California and South Florida. She now resides in Kentucky and writes full time.

As a former sales rep for a major manufacturer, she's traveled extensively throughout the US, and has a million stored memories to draw from for her stories. She spent her single years in San Francisco and considers that city one of America's treasures, comparable to no other city in the world. The books in her California Series, starting with *Winter Interlude*, are all set in the Bay Area.

Sandy is now an empty nester who has written almost two dozen novels. She strives to come up with fun characters—people you would love to call friends. We all know friends have their baggage and when we discover what makes them tick, we come to love them even more.

Whether contemporary romance, romantic suspense, historical, or time travel, Sandy always tries to weave a warm love story into her work, while providing enough twists and turns to entertain any reader.

Other Books by Sandy Loyd:

Contemporary Romance

CALIFORNIA SERIES: Books 1-3

Three couples find their way to love and happiness in these first three heartwarming stories all set in the San Francisco Bay area. Cozy up to the fire and fall in love with **WINTER INTERLUDE**. Experience a flirty, sexy & fun romance on a San Franciscan night in **PROMISES, PROMISES**. And read about **JAMES**, a man women love with one flaw - he can't commit.

A QUICKSTEP TO ROMANCE Book 4

Dirty dancing is the last thing on Mary Ann Murphy's mind, especially when the partner is Kyle Davidson, as flirty, fun, and sexy as they come. After all so was the last guy who broke her heart.

As the two step their way through the first class, an attraction flares between them, melting the ice around Mary Ann's heart. Still, she knows better than to fall for her sexy leading man with the killer gaze, who has made it clear he's not looking for long-term and she won't settle for anything less.

THE PROMISE OF TOMORROW Book 5

Unable to do anything to keep his best friend alive, he makes a promise to take care of his fiancée. Because of her fiancé's senseless death, she believes there is no tomorrow. He doesn't feel worthy of her and she doesn't believe her broken heart will ever heal.

SECOND CHANCES SERIES

TROPICAL SPICE Book 1 – Pepper Grady has vowed never to marry a man who can't remain faithful, especially someone like Ñico

Guerrero. Ñico doesn't believe in love, but he intends to marry Pepper to please his dying father. His plans go astray when the beautiful heiress seduces him instead, causing a major conflict between them. He's not sure he can promise what she desperately wants…a lifetime of love and fidelity.

Romantic Suspense

THE SIN FACTOR: BOOK ONE — DC BADBOYS SERIES

There is a thief in his midst. One of his highly sensitive prototypes has gone missing and in his search, he finds himself in the middle of a deadly game, where trust is a luxury he can't afford. The last person to have the devices is dead. His only link to the stolen property is the man's widow. When her life is put in danger, he works to uncover the truth before it's too late.

DEADLY MISCONCEPTIONS:

Private detective Lucy, struggling to shed her past as a thief and a runaway, finds herself neck-deep in danger—and unexpected romance—when she and her sexy nemesis Jack race to solve the mystery of a missing reporter.

SHATTERED DREAMS, a Romantic Suspense novel that takes place in the Miami-Ft. Lauderdale area.

Lies, betrayal, murder…all are the shards from his shattered dreams. Yet her lie of omission is the one piece that threatens to destroy him. Did she seduce him to gain his trust and then kill her estranged husband? Did her twin stab him? Or did they act together in a plot that's even too heinous to contemplate?

Time Travel/Historical

TIMELESS SERIES:

Three heartwarming romances…

TIME WILL TELL -Romance and adventure…and a trip to where an American tradition began when a she journeys back in time to Louisville, Kentucky just before the Kentucky Derby become a reality and stumbles upon her destiny. Unfortunately, he's in the wrong century.

GAMES: Twists and turns abound in this fun, fast-paced, suspense-filled mystery, where Giselle and Simon work to stay a step ahead of another, more devious game player intent on ending their journey to finding love and happiness.

TEMPTATION: Desperate to escape an abusive guardian, an English aristocrat sails to America disguised as a maid with secret plans to meet and marry her childhood sweetheart in order to regain her inheritance. Until she meets him, the one man who will ruin her best laid plans.